Look Here!

Written by Paul Brownie • Illustrated by Andrea Jaretzki

We might seem very, very tall
to a mouse.

We might seem very, very small
to a giraffe.

We might seem very, very heavy
to a bird.

We might seem very, very light
to an elephant.

We might seem very, very slow
to a cheetah.

We might seem very, very fast
to a snail.

We're always the same—
it just depends on who's looking!